What if the bus doesn't come?

Mark and Melanie prepare for school

Ginette Lamont Clarke
and Florence Stevens

Illustrations by
Odile Ouellet

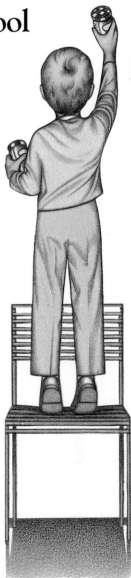

Tundra Books

Summer is over. Mark and Melanie are looking out the window. Tomorrow is the first day of school.

"When will the school bus come?" Mark says.

"The school bus will come for you after breakfast and bring you home for lunch," their mother answers.

"But what if the bus forgets to bring us home for lunch?" Mark asks.

"The bus won't forget you," their mother says.

"But, what if...?" Mark asks.

"Maybe we'd better take something for lunch," says Melanie.

Mark and Melanie go into the kitchen, where they make peanut butter sandwiches to take to school.

But Mark is still worried. "What if the bus doesn't come all afternoon?" he asks.

Melanie nods. "We'd better take something to play with."

Mark and Melanie collect some toys to take to school. Mark gets a ball and Melanie finds a book.

"Why do you want a book?" Mark asks. "They must have books at school."

"How do you know?" Melanie asks.

"We learn to read in school. They must have lots of books."

"I like this book," Melanie says. "You're taking your ball, I'm taking my book."

Mark puts his ball into a bag, but he is still worried. "What if the bus doesn't come? What if we're not home for supper?" he asks.

"We'd better take more food," says Melanie.

Mark and Melanie return to the kitchen to get more food.

"Let's take apples and bananas, and something to drink," Melanie says.

Mark takes down a jar of jam.

"You're not going to eat a whole jar of jam for supper?" Melanie asks.

"I like jam," Mark replies. But he is still worried. "What if the bus doesn't come after supper? What if we have to sleep at school?"

Melanie nods. "We'd better take our pajamas."

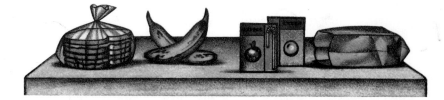

Mark and Melanie are in their room. Melanie pulls one of the blankets from her bed.

"I want my teddy bear," Mark says.

"And I want my puppy dog," says Melanie.

But Mark is still worried. "Do we have to brush our teeth?" he asks.

"I think so, and we need towels from the bathroom," replies Melanie.

They leave the bathroom, carrying blankets, towels, pajamas, toothbrushes, the teddy bear and the puppy dog.

But Mark is still worried. "What if the weekend comes and the bus still hasn't come?"

"We'd better take more toys," says Melanie.

Next, they go outside to play on the back porch.

"We only need one bike," says Melanie. "You can ride behind."

"No, I'll pedal," says Mark. "You ride behind." But then he wonders, "What if the bus doesn't come for a whole week?"

"Let's take Max and Minmin!" says Melanie.

Mark picks up Minmin and Melanie picks up Max.

"We'll need food for them," says Melanie.

"But are animals allowed in school?" Mark asks.

"I'm not sure," says Melanie. "Maybe we'd better leave them with Mom." She hugs the dog, "We can't take you to school, Max."

"Poor Minmin, we can't take you either," says Mark. But he is still worried. "What if winter comes and the bus still hasn't come for us?"

Melanie nods. "We'd better take our snowsuits."

Mark and Melanie go into the garage. Mark brings the snowsuits and skates while Melanie packs a shovel.

"I think we've got everything we need," says Melanie. "We have sandwiches, a book, a ball, a jar of jam, apples and bananas and something to drink, your teddy bear and my puppy dog, our toothbrushes, pajamas, blankets and towels, a bike, snowsuits, skates, and a shovel."

"And a toboggan," adds Mark.

The next morning, Mark and Melanie and their mother wait on the sidewalk for the school bus.

The bus arrives full of children. The driver opens the door and asks in surprise, "What in the world do you have there? Are you two coming to school or are you moving away?"

Melanie looks at the children on the bus. "We're coming to school," she answers.

Mark is still a little worried. He whispers to his mother, "Do you think she really will come to bring us home?"

"What do you think?" asks his mother.

Mark looks at the driver and the children. "I guess so," he says. "Let's go, Melanie."

"O.K.," says Melanie. "But let's take the sandwiches anyway."

As the bus drives away, Mark and Melanie look out the back window at their mother who now has to carry everything back into the house.

© 1990 Odile Ouellet, illustrations
© 1990 Ginette Clarke, Florence Stevens, text

Published in Canada by Tundra Books, Montreal,
Quebec H3G 1R4
Published in the United States by Tundra Books of Northern
New York, Plattsburgh, N.Y. 12901

ISBN 0-88776-251-4 hardcover
ISBN 0-88776-259-X softcover
Library of Congress Catalog Number: 90-70135

Design by Michael Dias

Canadian Cataloging in Publication Data

Stevens, Florence, 1928-
    What if the bus doesn't come?

Issued also in French under title: Et si l'autobus nous oublie?
ISBN 0-88776-251-4

    I. Clarke, Ginette, 1957- . II. Ouellet, Odile. III. Title.

PS8587.T4723W43 1990   jC813'.54   C90-090150-0
PZ7.S84Wh 1990

The publisher has applied funds from its Canada Council block
grant for 1990 toward the editing and production of this book.

Printed in Hong Kong by South China Printing Co. (1988) Ltd.